Put Beginning Readers on the Right Track with
ALL ABOARD READING™

Picture Readers—for Ages 3 to 6
Picture Readers have super-simple texts, with many nouns appearing as rebus pictures. At the end of each book are 24 flash cards—on one side is the rebus picture; on the other side is the written-out word.

Pre-Level 1—for Ages 4 to 6
First Friends, First Readers have a super-simple text starring lovable recurring characters. Each book features two easy stories that will hold the attention of even the youngest reader while promoting an early sense of accomplishment.

Level 1—for Preschool through First-Grade Children
Level 1 books have very few lines per page, very large type, easy words, lots of repetition, and pictures with visual "cues" to help children figure out the words on the page.

Level 2—for First-Grade to Third-Grade Children
Level 2 books are printed in slightly smaller type than Level 1 books. The stories are more complex, but there is still lots of repetition in the text, and many pictures. The sentences are quite simple and are broken up into short lines to make reading easier.

Level 3—for Second-Grade through Third-Grade Children
Level 3 books have considerably longer texts, harder words, and more complicated sentences.

All Aboard for happy reading!

For all the "Bosses" in my life, especially
Doug, Bob, Maureen, Judie, Margaret, Jane,
Cecilia, Katrina, Jenny, and Mario,
but not Sally Campbell.

Jennifer Smith-Stead, Literacy Consultant

Library of Congress Cataloging-in-Publication Data is available.

ISBN 0-448-42544-0 (pbk.)   A   B   C   D   E   F   G   H   I   J
ISBN 0-448-42618-8 (GB)   A   B   C   D   E   F   G   H   I   J

BARKERS

BOSS
FOR A DAY

by Tomie dePaola

Grosset & Dunlap • New York

MOFFAT · 1:02 P.M.

MORGAN · 1:12 P.M.

4

Moffie liked being the boss.
After all, she was ten minutes
older than Morgie.

"Morgie, don't wear that shirt,"
Moffie said.

"Wear this one."

"Morgie, you are always
reading that book,"
Moffie said.
"Try this one."

"Morgie, we are going
to play school now," Moffie said.
"I am the teacher.
You and Dolly are the class."
"But I don't want to play school,"
Morgie said.

Mama heard Moffie.

"You are being too bossy,"
she told Moffie.

"Let Morgie do what he wants."
Moffie thought about it.

At bedtime Moffie said,

"Morgie, I have a good idea.

Tomorrow you be the boss."

"But I don't know how,"
Morgie said.

"It is easy," Moffie said.

"I will show you.
Now go to sleep."

The next morning,
Moffie woke up Morgie.

"Get up, Morgie," Moffie said.

"It's time to be the boss."

Moffie picked up two skirts.
"Should I wear my blue skirt
or my pink skirt?"
she asked.

Before Morgie said a word,
Moffie said,
"I will wear my pink skirt."

Morgie and Moffie
sat down at the table
for breakfast.

"Morgie," Moffie said,
"you have to tell me
 to drink my milk!"
"Drink your milk," Morgie said.

"Do you want muffins or toast?"

Mama asked the twins.

"We want toast, Mama,"

Morgie said.

"No," Moffie said.

"We want muffins."

After breakfast,

Moffie asked Morgie,

"What are we going to do today?"

Morgie got his dinosaurs.

"Let's play," Morgie said.

"That is no fun," Moffie said.

She got Dolly.

"Now let's play."

So they did.

After lunch,

Billy came over.

"Morgie is the boss today,"

Moffie told Billy.

"We have to do everything he says."

"Let's play jump rope,"
Moffie said.

They played
jump rope.

"Let's play Follow the Leader,"
Moffie said.

They played Follow the Leader.

They played dress-up.

"Now let's have a tea party,"
Moffie said.

"I have to go home,"
Billy said.

At supper,
Moffie told Papa,
"Morgie was the boss <u>all</u> day.
I did everything he told me to.
Right, Morgie?"

After their baths,
the twins got ready
for bed.

"I had so much fun today, Morgie,"
  Moffie said.
"See? I told you it was easy
  to be the boss!"

But Morgie didn't hear Moffie.

He was fast asleep.

Wow! Moffie thought,

being BOSS really wore him out.